ALL
summer's fun

Written and Illustrated by Daniel Skalak

red
cygnet™
PRESS

San Diego, California

red cygnet™ PRESS

To my parents for always helping me out of the mud and
pointing me in the direction of the sunlight. – D.S.

Illustrations copyright © 2007 Daniel Skalak
Manuscript copyright © 2007 Daniel Skalak
Book copyright © 2007 Red Cygnet Press, Inc., 11858 Stoney Peak Dr. #525, San Diego, CA 92128

Cover and book design: Amy Stirnkorb

First Edition 2007
10 9 8 7 6 5 4 3 2
Printed in China

Library of Congress Cataloging-in-Publication Data

Skalak, Daniel.
All summer's fun / written and illustrated by Daniel Skalak. -- 1st ed.
p. cm.
Summary: Describes the many fun things that friends do over the long summer, from swimming at the pool and playing ball to camping out and staying up late.
ISBN-13: 978-1-60108-000-4 (hardcover)
ISBN-10: 1-60108-000-X (hardcover)
[1. Summer--Fiction. 2. Stories in rhyme.] I. Title.
PZ8.3.S6186Al 2007
[E]--dc22
2006016933

YEA!

School is all over
And Summer's begun
It's time to go crazy,
It's time to have fun!

No pens and no papers,
No teachers or rules,
Just late nights and sleep-outs
And acting like fools.

No alarm clock today
I'll wake when it's right
(And I'll go back to sleep
When it's real late at night!)

I'll make my own breakfast
As soon as I wake
A big scoop of ice cream,
Then a whole chocolate cake.

It's quite hot this morning
And I'd rather stay cool,
So I grab my striped towel
And head for the pool!

In a contest to see
Who can make the best splash
Tidal waves rise from
Brugo's big belly bash.

After swimming
     and splashing
For hours on end,
Brugo suggests
We add one more friend.

No street, ledge, or alley
Is left unexplored,
As we zip on to Nip's house
With our trusty skateboards.

We gather our pals
Before it gets dark,
We grab balls and bats,
And head to the park.

Nip in the outfield
And Brugo at first,
Salo's GRAND SLAM
Has made the ball burst!

We're halfway through summer
We're enjoying the shade,
We eat tons of hot dogs
And drink lemonade.

A big cardboard box
Is a great place to play,
When Grobin climbs in,
We'll make-believe
   there all day.

"We'll make this a ship
And head for high seas,
We'll swagger like pirates
And sing in the breeze."

When hunger sets in
It's time for a break,
I'll head to the fridge
For a big juicy steak.

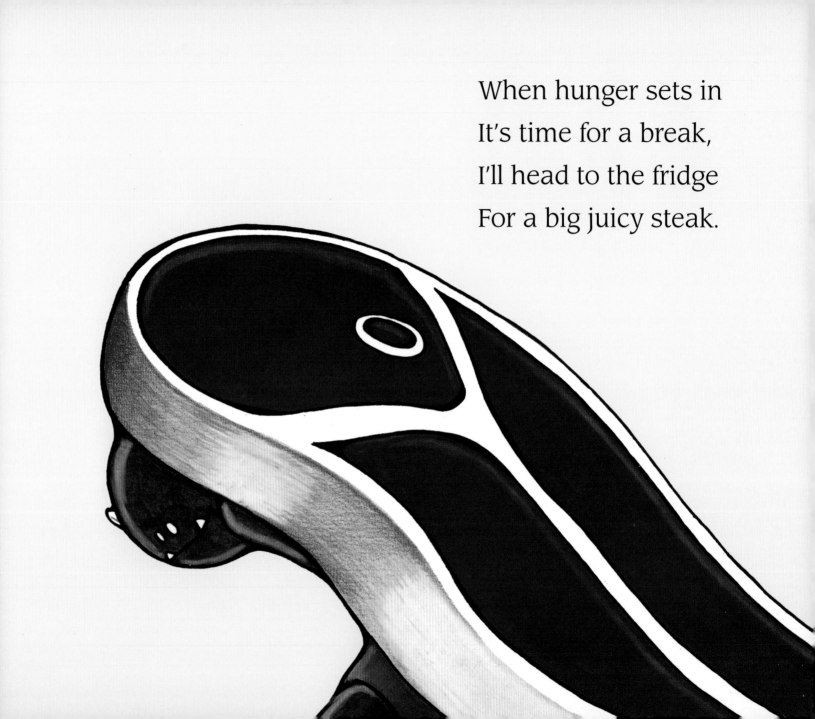

Comfortably full,
My face is a mess,
I fall fast asleep
I'm zonked, I confess.

I wake as my friends
Appear with their packs
They've got flashlights and tents
And tons of sweet snacks.

After stories of ghosts
At our favorite campground,
I'm not a bit scared
But...*wait*...
what's that sound?

Late in the summer,
I'm still going strong,
There's fun to be had
While the days are still long.

The weather is perfect
The clouds are like cotton
I laze in the grass,
My troubles forgotten.

A trip to the zoo
Is the perfect retreat,
The best things to see,
And the best things to eat.

My favorite displays
In the whole zoo to see
Are gorillas and monkeys
They remind me of me!

When the rain starts to pour

Forget the umbrella,

I'm a fun-in-the-mud and

A dirt kind of fella!

When I come through the door
My mother just shrieks,
"Look at that mess!,
'I'll have to wash you for weeks!"

As I climb into bed,

I think back on these days,

The pool and the tents,

And soaking in rays.

Then the cooler nights start
I need heavier clothes
(This causes a teardrop
To roll down my nose).

Now summer is over
And school is back in,
I find all my friends
Are still wearing a grin.

We talk about good times
All the things that we've done,
We laugh and agree that. . .